SCOOBY-DOO EXPLORES THE NEIGHBOURHOOD

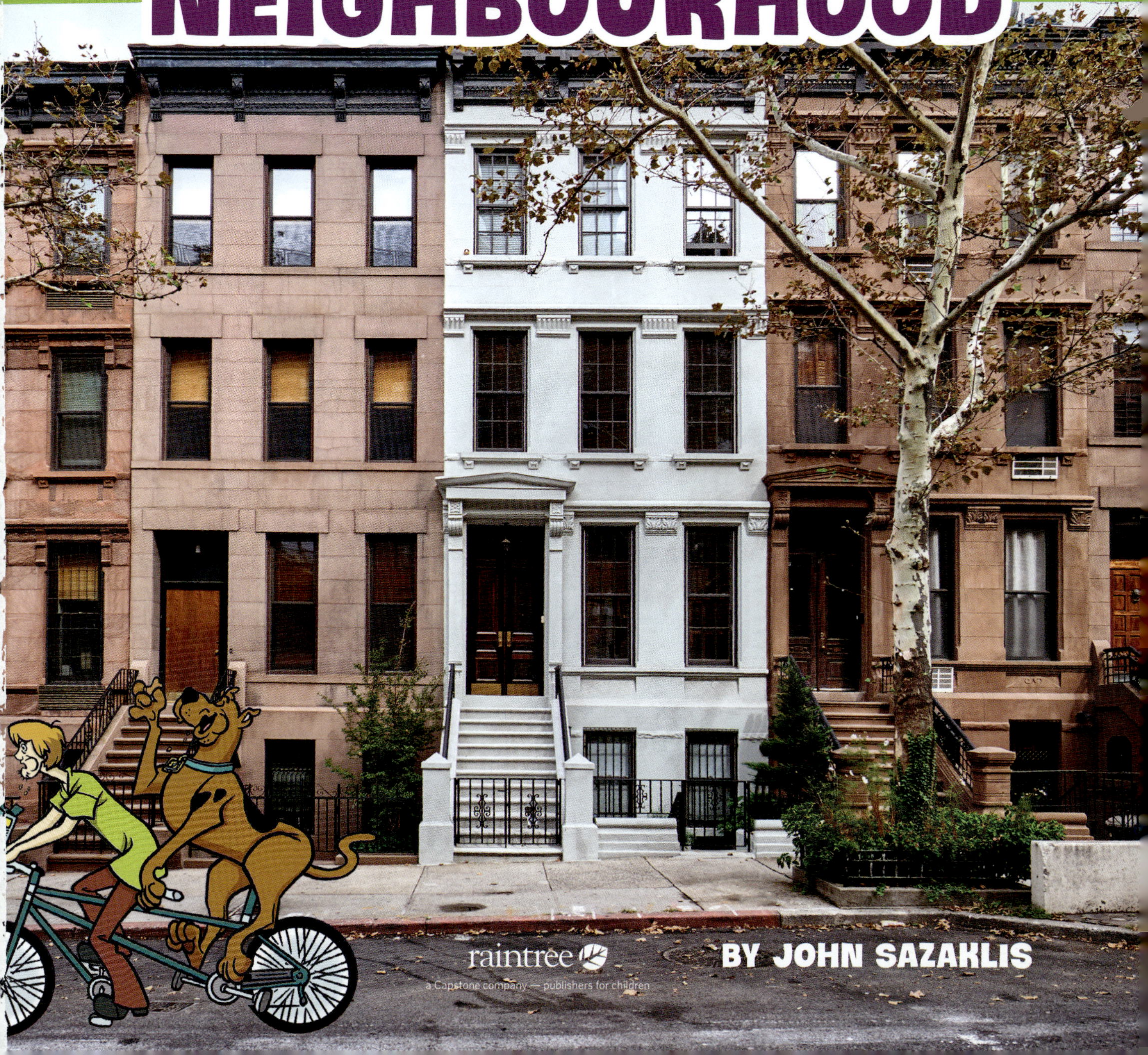

BY JOHN SAZAKLIS

raintree
a Capstone company — publishers for children

Raintree is an imprint of Capstone Global Library Limited, a company incorporated in England and Wales having its registered office at 264 Banbury Road, Oxford, OX2 7DY – Registered company number: 6695582
www.raintree.co.uk
myorders@raintree.co.uk

Copyright © 2025 Hanna-Barbera.
SCOOBY-DOO and all related characters and elements © & ™ Hanna-Barbera (s25)

The moral rights of the proprietor have been asserted. All rights reserved. No part of this publication may be reproduced in any form or by any means (including photocopying or storing it in any medium by electronic means and whether or not transiently or incidentally to some other use of this publication) without the written permission of the copyright owner, except in accordance with the provisions of the Copyright, Designs and Patents Act 1988 or under the terms of a licence issued by the Copyright Licensing Agency, 5th Floor, Shackleton House, 4 Battle Bridge Lane, London, SE1 2HX (www.cla.co.uk). Applications for the copyright owner's written permission should be addressed to the publisher.

ISBN 978 1 3982 5633 0

Editorial Credits
Editor: Christianne Jones; Designer: Bobbie Nuytten; Media Researcher: Rebekah Hubstenberger; Production Specialist: Whitney Schaefer

British Library Cataloguing in Publication Data
A full catalogue record for this book is available from the British Library.

Image Credits
Alamy: Len Collection, 19 (middle); Getty Images: Alexander Spatari, 9 (top right), Allison Joyce, 15 (middle), alvarez, 29 (middle left), Brian Kersey, 16, Caia Image, Cover (middle right), Cancan Chu, 15 (bottom), FrankvandenBergh, 22, Hulton Archive, 23 (middle), 31 (top), iStock/baona, 6, iStock/Dennis Swanson - Studio 101 West Photography, 21 (middle left), iStock/espiegle, 27 (top), iStock/felixmizioznikov, 25 (middle left), iStock/Gregor Inkret, 7 (middle), iStock/niknikon, 21 (middle), iStock/scaliger, 26, JGalione, 4 (top right), Justin Sullivan, 19 (bottom), Katrin Ray Shumakov, 3 (middle right), 24, manonallard, 25 (top), martin-dm, 3 (bottom left), 20, MesquitaFMS, 25 (middle right), Olaf Kruger, 27 (bottom), Putu Sayoga, 15 (top), SolStock, 3 (bottom middle), 30, Spencer Platt, 17 (top left), TommL, 2 (bottom left), 8, Topical Press Agency, 19 (top), WALTER ZERLA, 4 (bottom); Library of Congress: Prints and Photographs Division, 11 (top); Shutterstock: Africa Studio, 11 (bottom), Aleksandr Ryzhov, 17, Brian Goodman, Cover (top right), 1, Diane Bondareff, 13 (top right), DisobeyArt, 29 (top right), Drazen Zigic, 13 (middle right), 29 (top left), hxdbzxy, 9 (top right), Igor Bukhlin, 10, Josef Hanus, 2 (bottom right), 12, Kira_Yan, Cover (middle right background), kittirat roekburi, 28, Kzenon, 21 (top right), Lopolo, 14, MeganBrady, 27 (middle), Michaelpuche, 18, MirasWonderland, 23 (bottom), Niloo, 9 (middle right), Orhan Cam, 7 (top), Rawpixel.com, 13 (middle left), Rudmer Zwerver, 7 (bottom), Sheila Fitzgerald, 31 (bottom), Tatiana Migunova, Cover (bottom right), TongRoRo, 31 (middle), Viktoriia Hnatiuk, 9 (middle left), voronaman, 11 (middle), wavebreakmedia, 5 (middle); The New York Public Library: The Miriam and Ira D. Wallach Division of Art, Prints and Photographs, 23 (top)

A NEW NEIGHBOURHOOD

The Scooby-Doo gang is lost in a new neighbourhood!

A neighbourhood is an area in a town or city where a group of people live. Some neighbourhoods are big. Some are small. Some are old. Some are new.

Use the clues in the photos and text to guess each place the gang has discovered in the new community.

Scooby and Velma are in a building full of books. Looking for a spooky story or a mystery? An expert employee will lead the way. They will even let you borrow the books to read at home!

Velma delves into research on a computer.

Scooby is captivated by story time.

SCOOBY-DOO, WHERE ARE YOU?

The largest library in the United States is the Library of Congress in Washington DC.

Built in 859, the Al-Qarawiyyin Library in Morocco is the oldest one still open for business.

Real bats live in the Joanina Library in Portugal. They eat insects that damage book pages.

Ruh-roh! Scooby's run out of Scooby Snacks! Shaggy finds the perfect place to get some food. There are aisles and aisles filled with tasty treats and scrumptious snacks.

There are rows and rows of fruits and vegetables.

There is even a meat counter and a bakery section.

SCOOBY-DOO, WHERE ARE YOU?

WE ARE AT A SUPERMARKET!

Like, did you hear about the snowman looking for carrots? He was "picking" his nose!

Ree-hee-hee!

Piggly Wiggly was the first supermarket in the world. It opened in 1916 in Memphis, Tennessee, USA.

Self-service checkouts were invented in 1992.

The shopping trolley was invented in 1937. It has many names around the world, including cart and buggy.

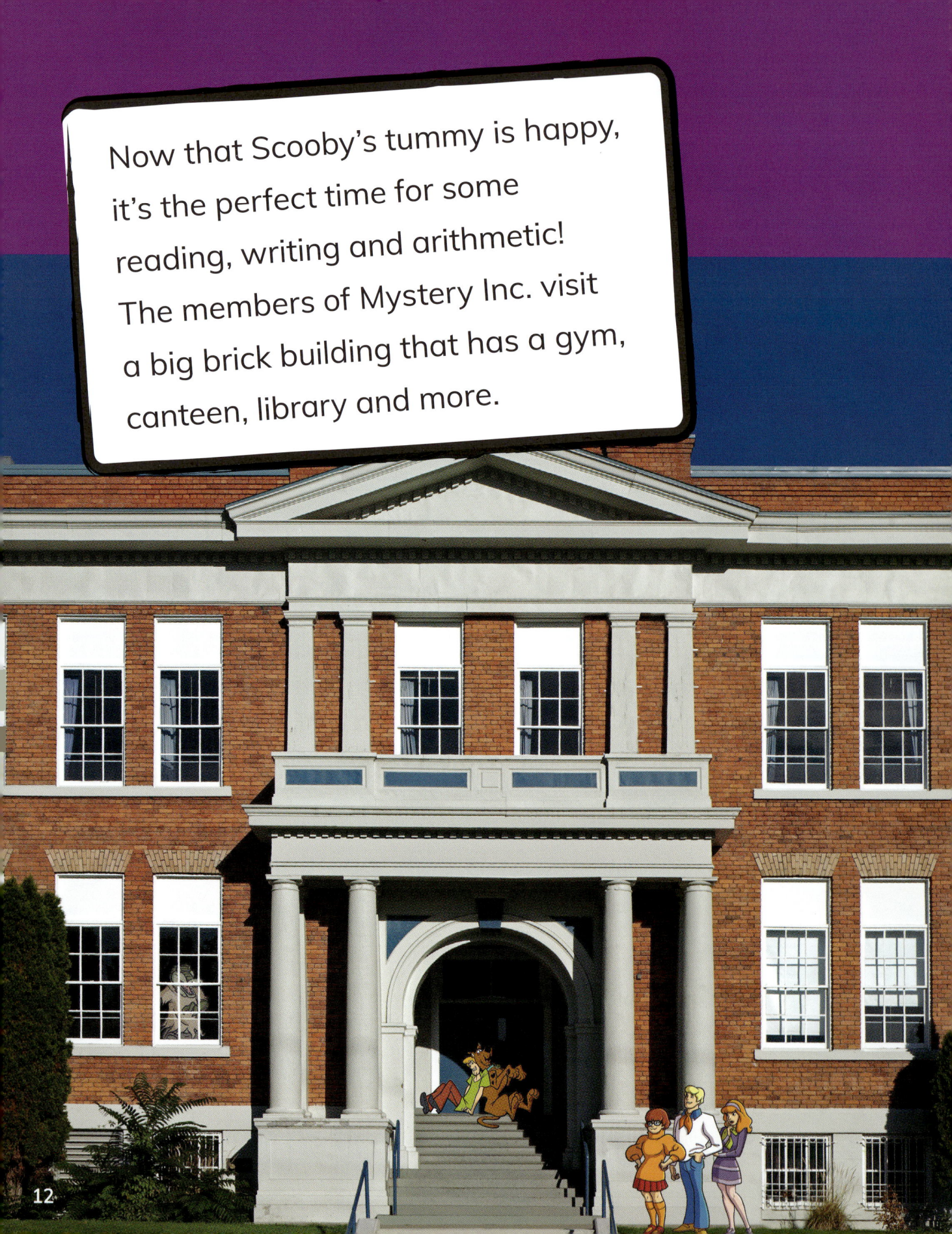

Now that Scooby's tummy is happy, it's the perfect time for some reading, writing and arithmetic! The members of Mystery Inc. visit a big brick building that has a gym, canteen, library and more.

Lockers line the long corridors.

Flyers about robotics, sports, theatre and more activities fill the noticeboards.

Classrooms are filled with eager students and excited teachers. They even voted Scooby to be teacher's pet!

SCOOBY-DOO, WHERE ARE YOU?

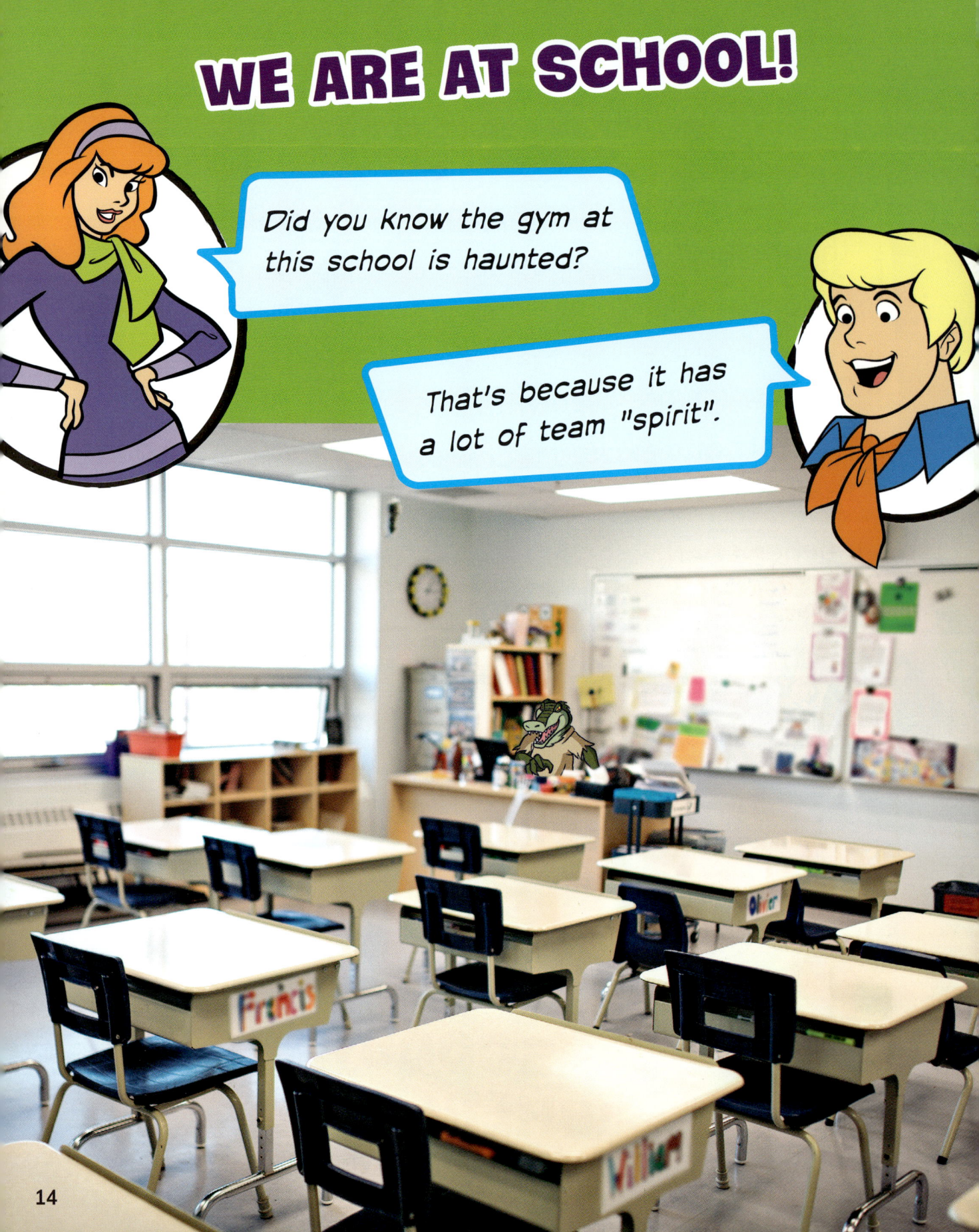

The Green School in Bali, Indonesia, is eco-friendly. It's made from bamboo, uses solar panels and has a hydro-powered generator.

Floating boat schools mean children can still go to class during big floods in Bangladesh.

The Dongzhong Cave School in China was open from 1984 to 2011.

After school, the gang finds a place that's filled with letters and parcels.

This busy building is a hub for all the mail in the neighbourhood. If you need to send something, this is the place to be!

Fred buys stamps while Shaggy takes a new passport photo. **Smile!**

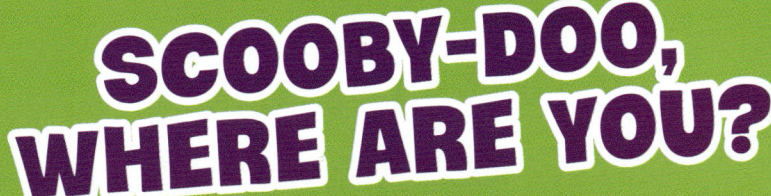

WE ARE AT THE POST OFFICE!

"What has more letters than the alphabet?"

"The Post Office!"

At one time, carts and horses were used to deliver letters and parcels.

In 1888, the US Post Office had an unofficial mascot – Owney the Dog!

Millions of pieces of mail are collected, sorted and delivered every day by Postal Services everywhere.

DING! DING! DING! As Scooby and his friends leave the post office, they hear an alarm. It's a call to action for trained people who help in emergencies.

They quickly put on all their gear to stay safe. Then they slide down the pole and pile into a big red engine. They hit the siren and the lights, and away they go!

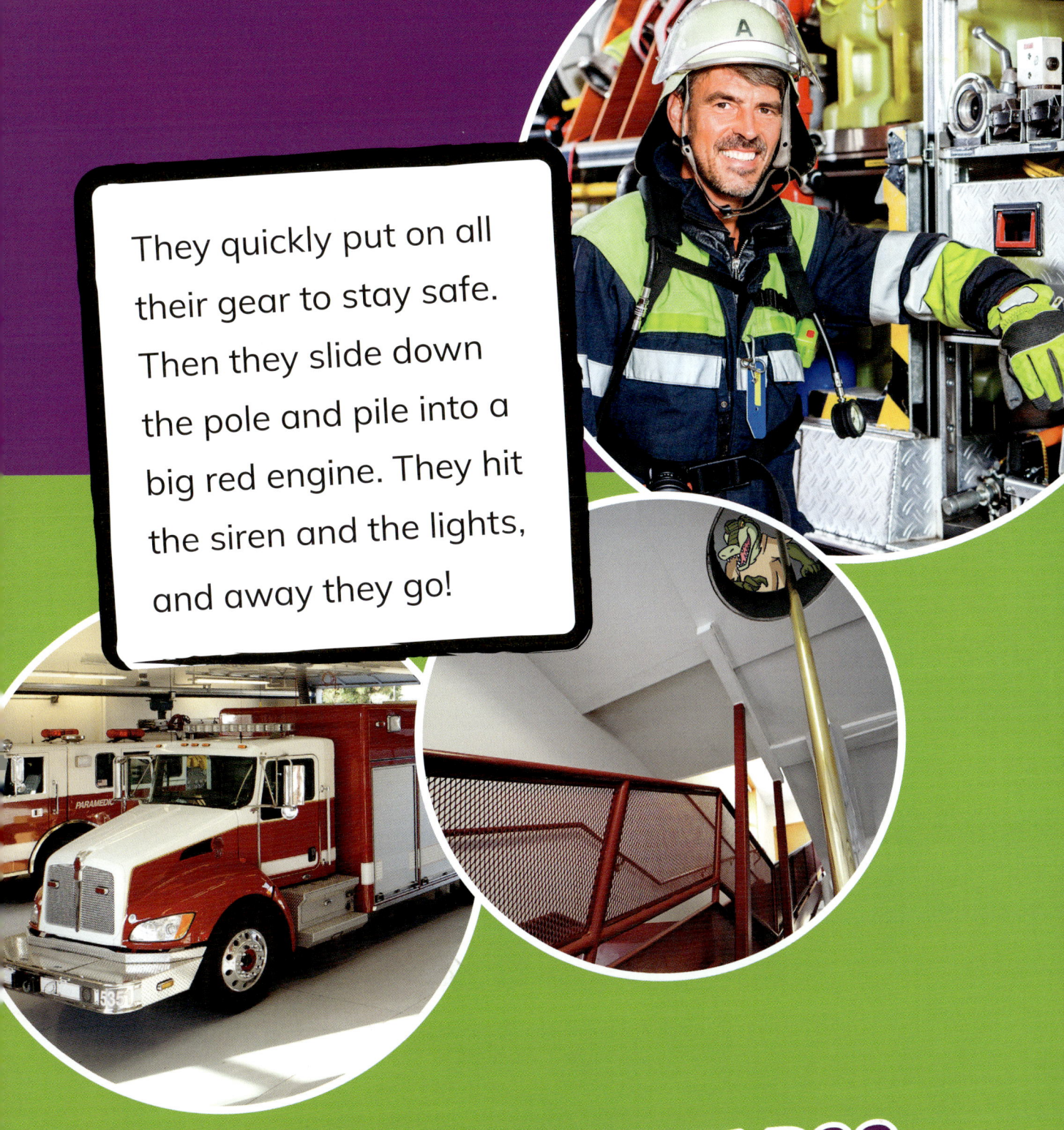

SCOOBY-DOO, WHERE ARE YOU?

Benjamin Franklin established the first US fire company in 1736.

In the 19th century, fire engines were pulled by horses.

Dalmatians helped firefighters in the US. They are known for their ability to calm down horses!

After all that excitement, the gang needs a break! They see a grassy field with lots of trees. A footpath surrounds the field.

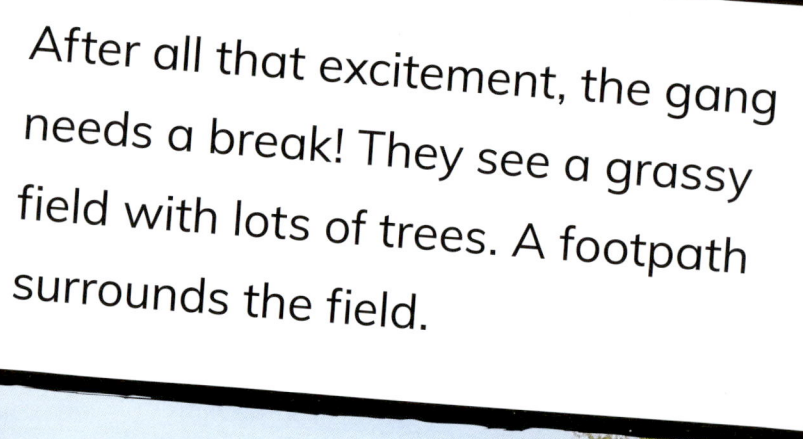

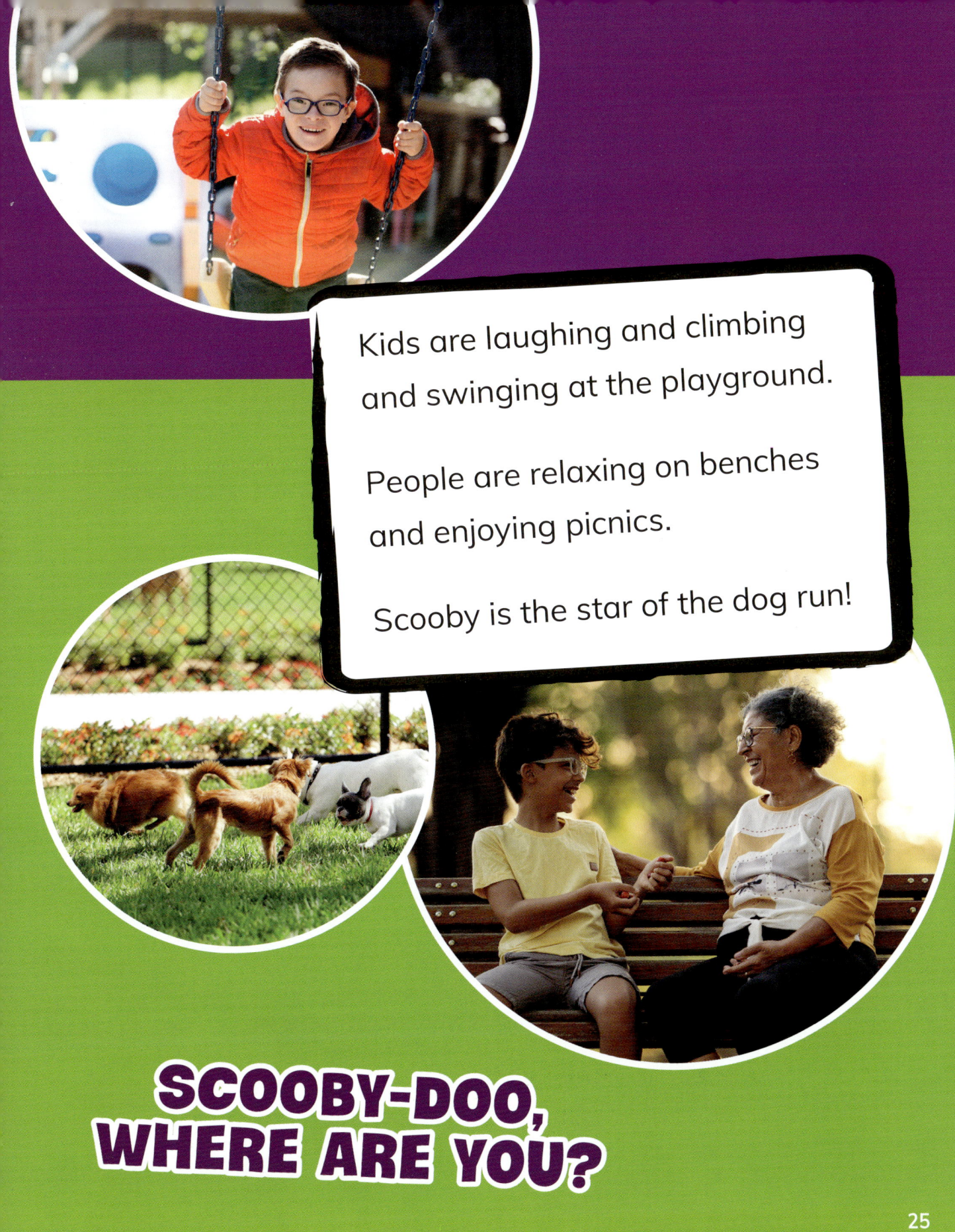

Kids are laughing and climbing and swinging at the playground.

People are relaxing on benches and enjoying picnics.

Scooby is the star of the dog run!

SCOOBY-DOO, WHERE ARE YOU?

Even though it's in New York City, USA, Central Park is bigger than some countries!

In 1872, Yellowstone Park in Wyoming, USA, became the first national park in the world.

Greenland's National Park is the world's largest.

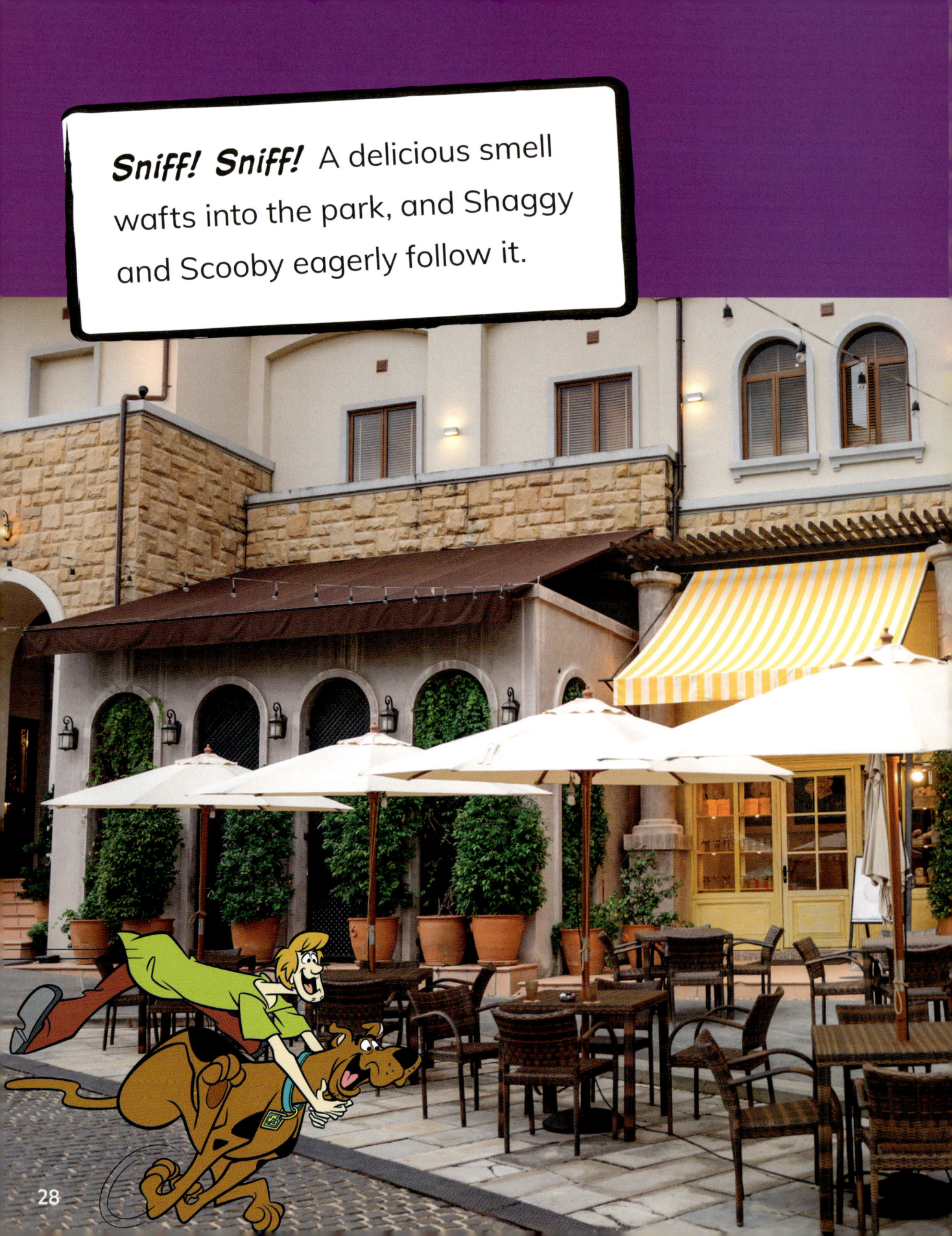

Sniff! Sniff! A delicious smell wafts into the park, and Shaggy and Scooby eagerly follow it.

Sparkling lights glow over a packed patio.

Tables and booths are filled with families and friends.

Waiters rush around taking orders and delivering food and drinks.

SCOOBY-DOO, WHERE ARE YOU?

Many people believe the first "modern" restaurant opened in 1765 in Paris, France.

The Union Oyster House in Boston is the oldest restaurant in the United States. It has been open since 1826.

White Castle was the first fast food restaurant chain. It opened in 1921.

Scooby-Doo and the Mystery Inc. gang explored every corner of a new neighbourhood, but they weren't alone! The Gator Ghoul wanted to explore a new neighbourhood too! Look through the book again and spot him hiding in each location.

ABOUT THE AUTHOR

John Sazaklis is a *New York Times* bestselling author with almost 100 children's books under his utility belt! He has also illustrated Spider-Man books, created toys for MAD magazine and written for the BEN 10 animated series. John lives in New York City, USA, with his super-powered wife and daughter.